Stinky Spike
the Pirate Dog

READ & BLOOM BOOKS

Agnes and Clarabelle
Agnes and Clarabelle Celebrate!

Stinky Spike the Pirate Dog
Stinky Spike and the Royal Rescue

Wallace and Grace Take the Case
Wallace and Grace and the Cupcake Caper

The Adventures of Caveboy
Caveboy Is Bored!

Stinky Spike
the Pirate Dog

illustrated by

Peter Meisel   Paul Meisel

BLOOMSBURY

NEW YORK   LONDON   OXFORD   NEW DELHI   SYDNEY

For Mom and Dad —Peter M.

For Pete, who wrote a really funny,
stinky book! —Paul M.

Text copyright © 2017 by Peter Meisel
Illustrations copyright © 2017 by Paul Meisel

First published in the United States of America in March 2017
by Bloomsbury Children's Books
www.bloomsbury.com

Bloomsbury is a registered trademark of Bloomsbury Publishing Plc

For information about permission to reproduce selections from this book, write to
Permissions, Bloomsbury Children's Books, 1385 Broadway, New York, New York 10018
Bloomsbury books may be purchased for business or promotional use. For information on
bulk purchases please contact Macmillan Corporate and Premium Sales Department at
specialmarkets@macmillan.com

Library of Congress Cataloging-in-Publication Data
Names: Meisel, Peter, author. | Meisel, Paul, illustrator.
Title: Stinky Spike the pirate dog / by Peter Meisel ; illustrated by Paul Meisel.
Description: New York : Bloomsbury, 2017.
Summary: When Spike finds himself adrift at sea he is rescued by a crew of surly pirates,
who spend their days hunting for treasure. Spike knows that he was meant to sniff out
treasure, but his sense of smell leads him to some unusual treasure.
Identifiers: LCCN 2015022815
ISBN 978-1-61963-778-8 (hardcover) • ISBN 978-1-61963-814-3 (e-book) • ISBN 978-1-61963-868-6 (e-PDF)
Subjects: | CYAC: Dogs—Fiction. | Smell—Fiction. | Pirates—Fiction. | Humorous stories. |
BISAC: JUVENILE FICTION / Readers / Chapter Books. | JUVENILE FICTION / Animals / Dogs. |
JUVENILE FICTION / Action & Adventure / Pirates. | JUVENILE FICTION / Humorous Stories.
Classification: LCC PZ7.1.M469 St 2017 | DDC [E]—dc23
LC record available at https://lccn.loc.gov/2015022815

Art created using pencil on Strathmore Bristol and colored digitally
Typeset in Century Schoolbook
Book design by Amanda Bartlett and Yelena Safronova
Printed in China by C&C Offset Printing Co Ltd, Shenzhen, Guangdong
1 3 5 7 9 10 8 6 4 2

All papers used by Bloomsbury Publishing, Inc., are natural, recyclable products
made from wood grown in well-managed forests. The manufacturing processes
conform to the environmental regulations of the country of origin.

Table of Contents

CHAPTER 1
SHIPYARD DOG

Spike the pup's story begins at a busy shipyard.

But, unlike most dog tales, Spike's tale starts with his nose.

Spike had a super sniffer. It was
the world's most powerful nose.
"I smell fresh puffer-fish pie,
three miles away," he'd yip.

"Grilled barracuda burgers, two beaches down," he'd yap.

"A couple of stink-bats, up in that tree!" he'd yowl.

"We don't smell any stink-bats," the other shipyard pups would cry.

What Spike loved the most were
the nastiest, ickiest, foulest stinks
he could sniff.

"*Yarf, yarf,*" yipped Spike with
joy. "Stale snapper scales, baking

on the beach! Guppy guts, piled in a heap! Fly-covered fish eggs, stuck in the seaweed! YUM! The shipyard is full of stinky smells today!"

But life on the docks wasn't all
fun and smells. Being a shipyard
dog was hard work.

All day long, the pups ran up and
down the docks. They protected

the ships' cargo left alone by the
sailors. They scared away the
seabirds that swooped in for fresh
fish and chased away the rats that
snuck onto ships.

Ships from across the world sailed into the shipyard. They brought new stinky smells from faraway lands. Spike wanted to stick his nose into all of them.

"Quit sniffing around!" the shipyard boss would yell. "Get back to work!"

"Aye, aye, Boss," Spike would reply. And back to work he'd scamper, yapping at rats and scattering the seabirds.

One morning, Spike sat on the dock with his nose to the wind.

"Mmm, mmm. I love the smell of rotten fish," he said.

The breeze shifted, and Spike caught an even more powerful stench.

"Codfish, catfish, AND big, fat tuna! That can mean only one thing!" Spike dashed to the edge of the dock. A ship was sailing in. It was the *Dandy Dogger*, the biggest fishing ship on the high seas.

Spike knew she would be full of fresh fish, and that meant seafood for dinner!

"*Ah-roo! Ah-roo*," Spike howled to alert the shipyard. "Ship ahoy!"

"All paws on deck," bellowed the boss. "Move your tails and get to work!"

The pups sprang to life as the *Dandy Dogger* sailed in. They grabbed the ropes and tied up the ship. They helped the fishermen unload barrels of fresh fish. And they guarded the day's catch of fish when the sailors were away.

The *Dandy Dogger* brought more than fish to the shipyard. She also brought flocks of hungry seabirds. Pelicans, razorbills, spoonbills, and gulls of all sizes circled overhead, looking for scraps.

"Shipyard dogs! Do not let these bird bandits steal a scrap of this fish!" shouted the boss.

"*CAW!*" squawked a hungry gull. "You yapping fur balls can't stop us!"

Spike guarded a barrel of blowfish. "Find your own fish, feather-necks," he growled.

But the birds were much too
hungry to be chased away so easily.
A group of angry gulls began
SQUAWKING and swooping and
pecking at Spike.

Spike was in trouble. "Scram, flappers!" he howled as he bolted at the birds.

But there was a patch of slippery, slimy seaweed on the dock. Spike's paws slid out from under him. He skidded off the edge of the dock.

SPLASH! Spike landed in the ocean.

Spike doggy-paddled toward shore, but the strong current pulled him out to sea.

"Bark! Bark! Help!"
howled Spike. But
no one could hear
him over the
noisy birds.

Finally Spike spotted an old
wooden bucket floating nearby. He
paddled toward it.

The bucket was covered with
barnacles. Rotten fish bits sloshed
around inside. Spike crawled in
and held on tight. Lucky for Spike,
the bucket was seaworthy.

CHAPTER 2
LOST AT SEA

Spike bobbed up and down in his bucket as it drifted out to sea. He watched the shipyard get smaller and smaller. Soon it was out of sight. All Spike could see was water in every direction. The hot sun beat down on Spike. The smelly fish scraps that once filled the bucket now covered his fur.

Spike stunk.

"*Woof!* This is the stinkiest I've ever been," he said.

Spike's stomach growled. "I wonder what the other pups are having for lunch," he thought. "Is it pricklefish pizza? Squid soup? Codfish cake?"

Suddenly, a dark fin appeared in the water in front of the bucket.

A second one popped up next to it.
"Sharks!" squeaked Spike, as two
hungry sharks swam slow circles
around him.

"Jumping jellyfish! You stink!
Are you a skunk?" asked the first
shark.

The second shark laughed.

"Look again! Skunks have a stripe.

Methinks this is a shaggy sea-pig.

But do sea-pigs smell like rotten

fish?"

"I could take a bite and find out," said the first shark, smiling a scary, sharky smile that showed hundreds of sharp teeth.

Then the second shark laughed a scary, sharky laugh. "What kind of smelly fur ball are you?"

"I'm a dog," whimpered Spike. "From the shipyard."

"You're a dogfish?" asked the second shark.

"If he were a dogfish, he'd be swimming with us," said the first shark. "He must be a fishdog!"

"No. I'm just a dog. Can you take me back to land?" asked Spike.

"Sorry, Fishdog," said the shark. "No can do. You stink so bad, you'll scare away our dinner!"

The sharks slipped under the water and swam away.

"What if the next sharks like to eat stinky dogs? How will I ever get home?" worried Spike.

It was a long night in the bucket.

The next morning, a strong blast of water jolted Spike awake. It sent him soaring through the air, and

he landed on the back of a giant

blue whale.

"Well, hello. You're a mighty

small dog for such a powerful

stench," said the whale.

"Well, you're a really large fish,"

said Spike.

"I'm not a fish," said the whale.
"But I swam a long way to find
you. I had to see what could cause

such a horrible stink. I thought you'd be a garbage boat."

"Can you take me to land?" asked Spike.

"I'm sorry, Stink-dog, I live way out in the deep ocean. Land is no place for a blubbery fellow like me," said the whale. Then the whale took a deep, deep, deep breath and dove back under the water.

"Wait! How will I ever get home?" cried Spike.

But the whale was gone.

"Ahoy!"

Spike's ears perked up.

"Ahoy! You there!"

Spike looked around. It was a ship!

"*Yip! Yarf!* Over here!" barked Spike, waving his paws.

The ship sailed toward Spike. As it got closer, Spike saw a flag flying from the top of the mast.

"Shiver me sniffer," said Spike to himself. "Pirates!"

The pirates on the deck of the *Driftwood* stared at the pup in the bucket. They didn't know what to think.

"*Arrrgh*, is it a mermaid with dog hair?" asked the first mate, Zelda.

"No. You must be wearing your patch over the wrong eye again. It's a fuzzy bucket with ears," said Zip, the pirate monkey.

"*Arrrgh!* It's a dog *in* a bucket," said Captain Fishbeard, looking through his scope. "But what's he doing out here?"

"Well, he's sailing a mighty sorry ship," said Zelda.

"Should we bring him in?" asked Zip.

"Aye. It's the code of the sea to rescue castaways who are lost at

sea. Even pirates must follow the code. Bring him aboard," said Fishbeard.

Zip tossed a line to Spike. The pirates pulled him onto the deck of the *Driftwood*.

"Crusty clam shells! This sea dog stinks worse than rotten anchovies." Zip gagged.

"Or spoiled sardine stew!" Zelda choked.

"Blimey, that's quite a stench. What be your name, mutt?" Fishbeard scowled.

"Spike," squeaked the pup.

"You're no ordinary Spike. You be STINKY SPIKE! *Arrrgh!*" said Fishbeard, holding his nose.

CHAPTER 3
SNIFFING FOR TREASURE

Captain Fishbeard and his crew were known by every pirate who sailed the high seas as a blundering bunch. They never did anything right. In fact, they'd never even seen real treasure.

"Captain, thank you for the rescue. Can you take me home?" asked Spike.

"*Arrrgh!* Sorry, Stinky Spike, but we cannot take you home. We be looking for treasure," said Fishbeard.

"Well, maybe I can help," said Spike.

"You think *you* can help us find treasure? You're nothing but a bucket-sailing, foul-smelling sea mutt. What do you know about finding treasure?" Fishbeard laughed.

"I can *smell* treasure. I have the best sniffer on the seven seas. If I

find you treasure, will you take me home?" answered Spike.

Fishbeard agreed. "Sniff us some good loot, and we'll take you home."

Spike sniffed and sniffed. The *Driftwood* sailed on.

To pass the time, Captain Fishbeard sang pirate songs. Zip clapped and danced along.

"Yo ho, yo ho, a smelly mate he be."

"He'll lead us all to treasure."

"And then we'll shout . . . And then we'll shout . . . uh . . . er . . ."

"Stinky!" sang Zip.

"Blast it!" bellowed Captain Fishbeard. "Quit your laughin', you fool. I don't see you making up

pirate tunes or finding us any
treasure."

He glared at Zip, who was
already rolling on the deck
laughing.

Suddenly, Spike felt a whoosh of
wind.

"I've never smelled anything like this before," Spike barked.

"*Arrrgh*," hollered Fishbeard. "You'd best not be pulling me wooden leg, Stinky Spike."

"No, sir! It's the smell of real treasure!" yipped Spike. "And it's coming from that direction!"

Zelda followed Spike's orders and
steered the *Driftwood* into Jellyfish
Bay. In the middle of the bay sat
an empty ship.

"The treasure is on that ship. I
can smell it," said Spike.

"It doesn't smell like treasure to
me," said Zip.

"That is one shabby-looking ship," said Zelda.

"*Arrrgh!* And no pirates are on deck," said Fishbeard, drawing his sword. "Maybe it's a ghost ship! Crew, prepare for a fight!"

Zelda brought the *Driftwood* alongside the ship.

"Attack!" ordered Fishbeard as he charged ahead.

Spike and the pirates jumped onto her deck.

"*Arrrgh!* There's nobody here," shouted Zelda.

Fishbeard and Stinky Spike searched below the main deck.

"The treasure is down here, I can smell it," barked Spike.

Spike charged into the main hold. In the middle of the room was a heap of giant sacks!

"Treasure!" barked Spike, tearing one bag open with his teeth.

It was filled with sweaty pirate socks, stinky pirate underwear, and salt-stained pirate shirts.

"Here is your treasure, Captain Fishbeard. I bet the smelly socks are worth the most," said Spike proudly.

"Blast! This is no treasure. This be a laundry ship!" spat Fishbeard.

Zip burst into laughter. Captain
Fishbeard's face grew red with
rage. He stormed off, mumbling
pirate curses about smelly socks
and underwear.

"I don't understand. This smells like treasure to me. I'd better sniff real treasure soon, or Fishbeard will make me walk the plank," Spike said to himself.

That night, while the pirates were all sleeping, Spike aimed his

mighty sniffer into the air, hoping
to smell something good. Hours
passed. Then a strange sea breeze
brought Spike a whiff of something
he'd never sniffed before.

"Is *this* the treasure?" wondered Spike. He took the wheel and steered the *Driftwood*, using his snout to guide the way.

Spike sailed through the night, following the strange odor. As the sun rose, Spike saw palm trees ahead. The scent was coming from a tiny island.

Spike hopped overboard and paddled to shore.

He trotted along with his nose to

the ground, sniffing for

the source of the stink.

"Here!" barked Spike. He started

digging. Sand flew all around him.

Finally, there was a loud

CLUNK!!!

"It's a wooden chest," cried
Spike. He clawed at the lid, but it
was too thick. He bit the lock with
his teeth, but it was too strong. He
tugged on the chest, but it wouldn't
move.

At last, the pirates found Spike on the beach.

"Stinky Spike, this had better be real treasure!" said Zelda.

"*Arrrgh*, don't just stand there! Get this chest out of the ground!" commanded Fishbeard.

"Heave, ho. Heave, ho," sang the pirates, lifting the chest.

Captain Fishbeard cracked the rusty lock off the chest with his sword. The lid popped open . . .

"Cheese!?!" exclaimed Captain Fishbeard. "The chest be full of cheese! Moldy cheese is not treasure! Stinky Spike, you'll walk the plank for this trick."

Spike was confused. "How can this stinky cheese possibly not be treasure? It is the best, stinkiest smell I've ever sniffed!"

"This dog is bad luck. We should leave him on this island and be done with the smelly mutt," said Zelda.

Suddenly Zip squealed with joy. He reached underneath the cheese and pulled out something shiny . . .

"TREASURE!!!" yelled Captain
Fishbeard, dancing a happy pirate
jig.

Spike's super sniffer had found the long-lost treasure of the famous pirate-chef, Captain Cook. Buried beneath the moldy cheese were gold cups, forks, and spoons. There were silver frying pans and plates!

Captain Fishbeard and his crew had finally found treasure! And Spike had a new favorite stink: moldy, green cheese!

"You're a true pirate, Stinky Spike! How about you join my crew?" sang Fishbeard.

"Aye, aye, Captain Fishbeard. A pirate's life smells good to me!" said Spike.

"*Arrrgh*, then it's settled," said Fishbeard. "STINKY SPIKE, THE PIRATE DOG you be!"

Peter Meisel has been writing and illustrating since he was old enough to hold a crayon. He lives in Brooklyn, New York. *Stinky Spike the Pirate Dog* and *Stinky Spike and the Royal Rescue* are his first two children's books.

Paul Meisel lives in Newtown, Connecticut, with his wife and labradoodle, Coco, who was the inspiration for his two early readers, *See Me Dig* and the Geisel Honor–winning *See Me Run*. Paul is also the author/illustrator of *Good Night, Bat! Good Morning, Squirrel!* and has illustrated more than 70 books, including the bestselling I Can Read *Go Away, Dog*; *Run for Your Life!: Predators and Prey on the African Savanna*; and several Let's-Read-and-Find-Out Science books.

www.paulmeisel.com